No Tooting at Tea

No Tooting at Tea

by Alastair Heim   Illustrated by Sara Not

Clarion Books
HOUGHTON MIFFLIN HARCOURT
Boston   New York

Clarion Books
3 Park Avenue
New York, New York 10016

Clarion Books is an imprint of Houghton Mifflin Harcourt Publishing Company.

www.hmhco.com

The illustrations in this book were created in pencil and Photoshop.
Hand-lettering by Leah Palmer Preiss
The text was set in ITC Berkeley Old Style.

Library of Congress Cataloging-in-Publication Data
Names: Heim, Alastair, author. | Not, Sara, illustrator.
Title: No tooting at tea / Alastair Heim ; illustrated by Sara Not.
Description: Boston ; New York : Clarion Books, Houghton Mifflin Harcourt, [2017] | Summary: While trying to teach her younger sisters proper etiquette for a tea party, a young girl is distressed to hear a rude sound repeated.
Identifiers: LCCN 2015041141 | ISBN 9780544774742 (hardcover)
Subjects: | CYAC: Etiquette—Fiction. | Sisters—Fiction. | Tea—Fiction. | Parties—Fiction. | Flatulence—Fiction.
Classification: LCC PZ7.1.H4448 No 2017 | DDC [E]—dc23
LC record available at https://lccn.loc.gov/2015041141

Manufactured in China
SCP 10 9 8 7 6 5 4 3 2 1
4500638599

For my beautiful kiddos.
You make life a toot.
—A.H.

For Chiara, my inspiring
little muse.
—S.N.

Welcome to my tea party.

TEA PARTY →

Before we begin,
we must go over the rules
so that EVERYTHING goes perfectly.

Rule #1

Manners are very important at tea.
When you ask for lemon or a sugar cube,
you must say please and—

No. I didn't toot.
I think it was Mr. Train.

No.

Mr. Train's whistle is broken.

There is *no* tooting at tea.

Rule #2

Place a napkin neatly in your lap before pouring your—

No.
Owls don't toot, they hoot.

There is *NO* tooting at tea.

Rule #3

When you drink tea,
you must sip it, not—

Okay, NOW who tooted?

I think it was Mr. Trumpet.

No.

It wasn't Mr. Trumpet.

He is not one to toot his own horn.

Very well.

If no one will tell me who keeps tooting,

I have no choice but to cancel tea.

Good day.

TOO

Oh!
As I was
saying…

Rule #4

There is no tooting at tea...

...unless you are the teakettle, letting me know that the water is ready for tea.

Now then,
let's have tea.

That's okay....

You never said there was
no tooting AFTER tea.

TOOT!

Afterword

Tea has been enjoyed by grownups and children of all ages for thousands of years. It all started in China, where people loved drinking tea so much that news of it spread all over the world to places like Japan, India, Portugal, and Greece. But it wasn't until tea reached Great Britain that tea parties (both proper and improper) *really* took off. Tea is so popular today that there are more than a thousand kinds to choose from.

Making tea is easy, as long as you have the right tools and an adult to help. Tea leaves are what give tea its flavor and come both loose and in bags. While loose tea leaves are preferred by the most proper of tea-party patrons, they can be very messy. Bagged tea is more popular and much easier to use—but both methods make wonderful tea.

A teakettle boils hot water on the stove, and once it starts *TOOTING,* the water is ready to go into the teapot for serving. As soon as the tea leaves—either loose or bagged—are placed either into each teacup or into the teapot, the host pours in the hot water and removes the leaves after a few minutes; then the tea party can begin.

TREATS

TEA BAG

LOOSE TEA LEAVES

TEAPOT

TEAKETTLE

There are many ways to drink tea, all of them delicious. You can drink it hot or cold, with or without milk or a squeeze of lemon (but *never* with milk AND lemon—yuck!), and you can even sweeten the tea by adding honey or as many spoonfuls of sugar as you like (not *too* many!). For a bit of extra tea-party sweetness, use sugar cubes instead and watch them magically disappear into the tea!

As any proper tea-party host knows, nothing goes better with tea than a little something to nibble on. And the possibilities are endless! You can serve sweet and savory delights such as cookies, cakes, pies, muffins, croissants, doughnuts, candies, biscuits and jams, breads, scones, crackers, veggies, and even tiny cucumber sandwiches (if you so desire). There are no official rules for what treats you should serve your tea-party guests, but whatever you decide, just make sure they're scrumptious.

LEMON

SUGAR CUBES

HONEY

Honey

MILK

DRINK ME